GRANDMA'S RECORDS

ERIC VELASQUEZ

SCHOLASTIC INC.

New York   Toronto   London   Auckland   Sydney
Mexico City   New Delhi   Hong Kong   Buenos Aires

Book design by Diane Hobbing/Snap-Haus Graphics.

Credit for the song produced on page 31 is as follows: "En mi Viejo San Juan."
Words and music by Noel Estrada. Copyright © 1965. (Renewed) by Onyx Music Sales Corporation.
All rights administered by Music Sales Corporation (ASCAP). International Copyright Secured.
All rights reserved. Reprinted by permission.

The painting of the album cover for the record *Cortijo y Su Combo* is based on the original album released by Seeco Records, Inc.

All rights reserved. Published by Scholastic Inc, 557 Broadway, New York, NY 10012,
by arrangement with Walker Publishing Company, Inc.

Printed in the U.S.A.

ISBN-13: 978-0-545-10139-4
ISBN-10: 0-545-10139-5

4 5 6 7 8 9 10   40   17 16 15 14 13 12 11 10

Para mi abuela Carmen Maldonado (1909–1983), esta canción es para ti.

(For my Grandmother Carmen Maldonado [1909–1983], this song is for you.)

Every year, right after the last day of school, I'd pack a suitcase with my cool summer clothes, my favorite toys, and a sketchbook. Then my dog, Daisy, and I were off to Grandma's apartment in El Barrio. Because my parents worked, Grandma's apartment was my summer home.

From the time my parents dropped me off until the day they picked me up, Grandma wrapped me in her world of music.

Sometimes when she played a record, we would dance together. Other times, she would dance alone and tell me her stories about growing up in Puerto Rico.

When Grandma played a merengue from the Dominican Republic, her hips would sway from side to side. As her favorite salsa record played, she'd say, "Just listen to that conga," while she played an imaginary drum.

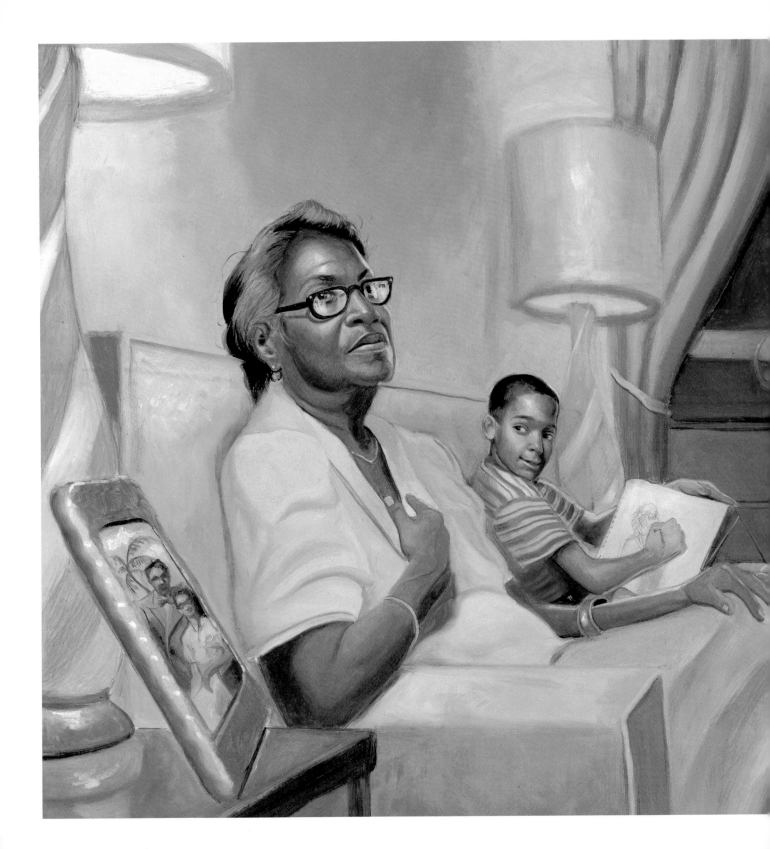

Grandma liked all types of music. But one record was very special to her. Whenever she played it, she would put her hand over her heart and close her eyes as she sang along. When it was over, Grandma would sometimes sit quietly, thinking about Grandpa and the old days in Santurce, her hometown.

"Sometimes," Grandma said, "a song can say everything that is in your heart as if it was written just for you."

My favorite days were the ones when Grandma would tell me, "You pick the records today." No matter what I would choose, Grandma would always say, *"Siempre me gusta tu selección."* (I always like your selection.)

Sometimes I would sneak in Grandma's special song just to watch her put her hand over her heart and sing.

Then she'd always ask, *"¿Cómo tú sabes?"* (How did you know?)

If it was too hot to go outside, I'd spend hours looking through all of Grandma's album covers. I'd pick out my favorites and make sketches of the art. As I drew, I could see the record covers coming to life and the bands performing right there in Grandma's living room.

Grandma never went to any nightclubs to see her favorite bands perform. She was happy just to stay home with me and listen to her scratchy records. But Santurce was home to hundreds of musicians, and she knew a lot of the people who played on the records.

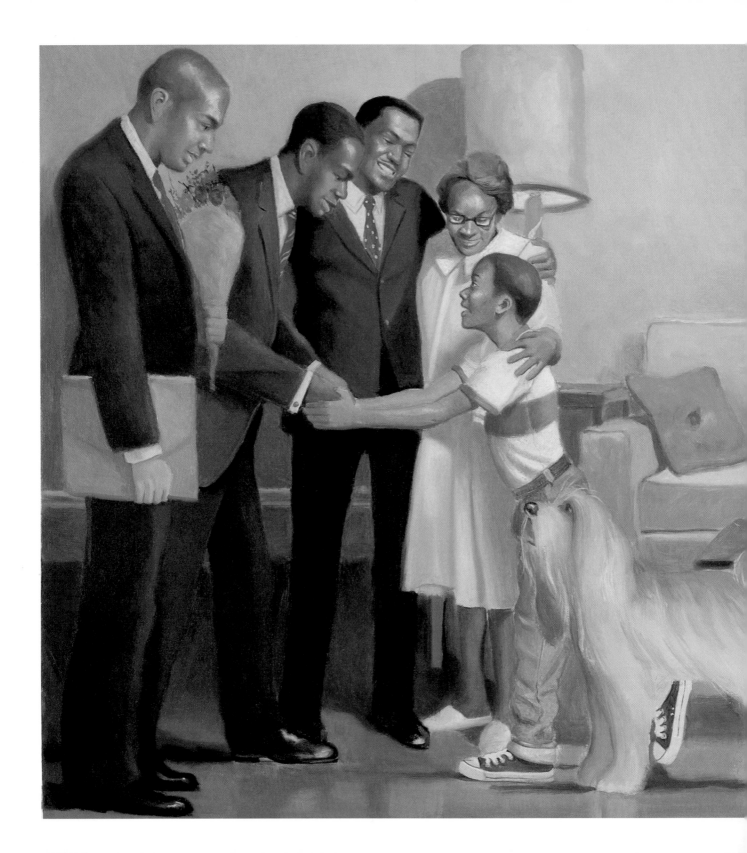

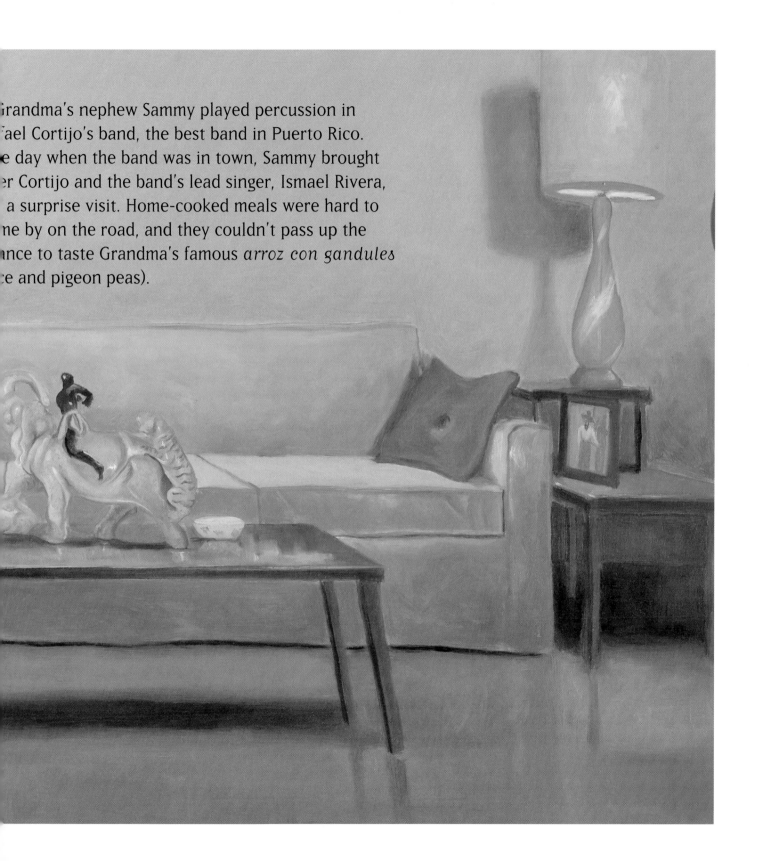

Grandma's nephew Sammy played percussion in
Rafael Cortijo's band, the best band in Puerto Rico.
One day when the band was in town, Sammy brought
over Cortijo and the band's lead singer, Ismael Rivera,
for a surprise visit. Home-cooked meals were hard to
come by on the road, and they couldn't pass up the
chance to taste Grandma's famous *arroz con gandules*
(rice and pigeon peas).

While eating dessert, Sammy had another surprise for Grandma: two tickets to the band's first New York concert, and their brand-new record, which wasn't even in the stores yet. I raced over to the record player, thrilled to be the first New Yorker to hear their latest music.

The next day, Grandma and I spent all day shopping
for clothes to wear to the show.

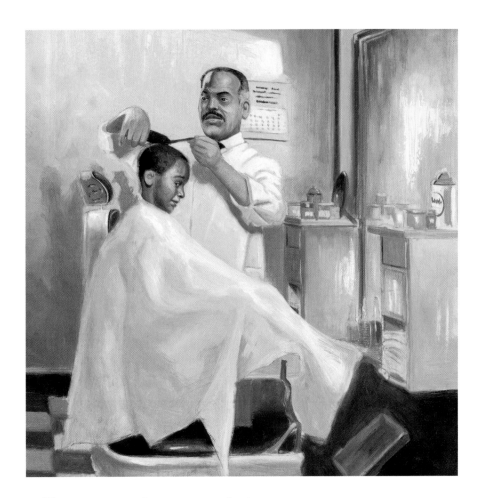

She even made me get a haircut.

The theater was all the way up in the Bronx. We took the subway there, and Grandma was nervous during the whole ride. When we got to the theater, we walked past the long line of people and went right inside because of our special tickets. The theater was bigger than all the movie theaters I had ever gone to.

The band made a spectacular entrance. Suddenly the
theater went dark, tiny lights glittered, and a loud siren
filled the air. I heard Grandma gasp, "¡Ay, Dios mío!"
(Oh my god). She thought something was wrong. The
darkened stage seemed to fill with people running back
and forth in confusion. Next, everything went dark
again, and a loud and steady conga beat began BOOM
BAK BOOM BAK BOOM BAK. Then the lights came on
with a loud BOOM, and the band began to play the
song "El Bombón de Elena" ("Elena's Candy").

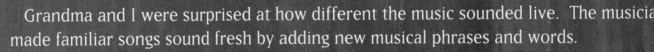

Grandma and I were surprised at how different the music sounded live. The musicia
made familiar songs sound fresh by adding new musical phrases and words.

Before the last song began, Ismael said, "This one goes out to Carmen," and he point
to Grandma as he sang her special song. I looked at her as she put her hand over her
heart, raised the other hand, closed her eyes, and began to sing along. Ismael was
singing to my grandma! Then I looked around and realized that everyone in the theat
had their hands over their hearts too.

After the show we went backstage. I asked Ismael how he knew about Grandma's song. He explained that the song was about coming to a new country and having to leave those you love behind. People put their hands over their hearts to show that their hearts remain in Puerto Rico even though they may be far away. Now I understood why Grandma's song was special to so many people.

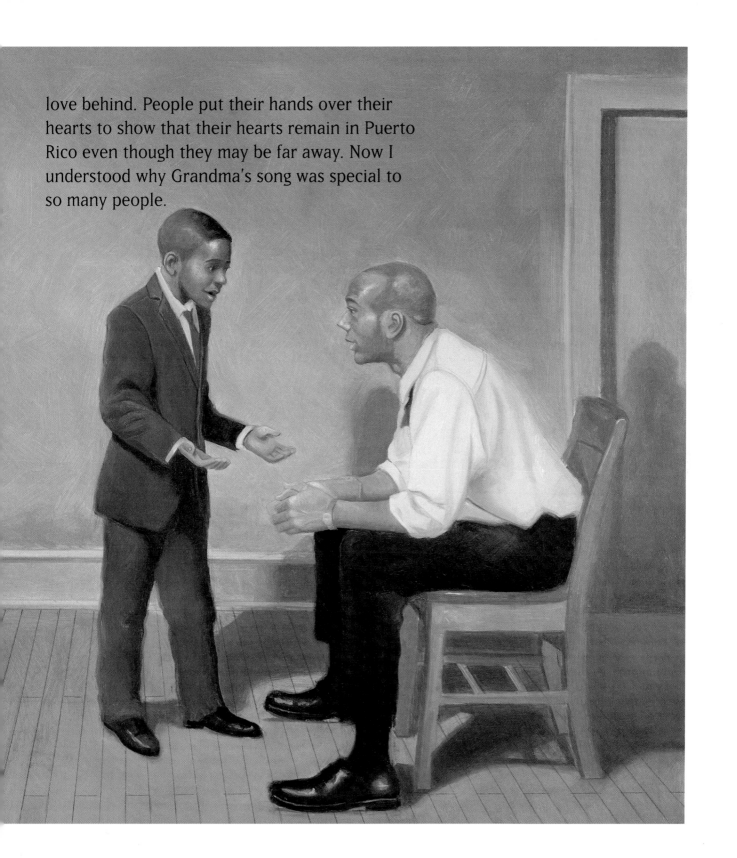

Over the next days and weeks, Grandma and I put on our own shows imitating Cortijo's band. Grandma wished such a special night had been captured in a recording so that she could listen to it again and again. But even then I knew that a concert is so special because it leaves you with the memory of a magical moment in time.

As I got older, I started bringing over my records to play for Grandma—Brazilian music, jazz, and even rap. She loved listening to it all.

Even now, when I'm playing CDs in my studio, I imagine I'm back in Grandma's living room and she turns to me and says, "You be the DJ today. *Siempre me gusta tu selección.*" And as I work, Grandma's special song surrounds me.

Grandma's special song in Spanish and in English.

"En mi viejo San Juan," by Noel Estrada

En mi viejo San Juan cuantos sueños forjé en mis años de infancia.
Mi primera ilusión y mis cuitas de amor son recuerdos del alma.
Una tarde me fui hacia extraña nación pues lo quiso el destino pero mi
corazón se quedó frente al mar en mi viejo San Juan.
Adiós, Borinquen querida, adiós, mi perla del mar.
Me voy, pero un día volveré, a buscar mi querer, a soñar otra vez
en mi viejo San Juan.
Pero el tiempo pasó y el destino tronchó mi terrible nostalgia y no pude
volver al San Juan que yo amé, pedacito de patria.
Mi cabello blanqueo, ya mi vida se va, ya la muerte me llama y no quiero
morir alejado de ti, Puerto Rico del alma.

"In My Old San Juan"

In my old San Juan I grew up with so many dreams.
My first illusion and anxieties about love are all soulful memories.
One evening I left for this foreign land, it was destiny's will, but my heart
remained by the seashore of my old San Juan.
Good-bye, beloved Borinquen, good-bye my pearl of the sea.
I'm leaving, but someday I will return, to look for my love, to dream once again,
in my old San Juan.
But time passed and destiny eased my homesickness, and I could not return to
the San Juan that I loved, little piece of my native land.
My hair has turned white as my life slowly fades, death seems to call, and I
don't want to die separated from you, Puerto Rico of my soul.

♫ ⦿ ♪

About Rafael Cortijo, Ismael Rivera, and Sammy Ayala

Rafael Cortijo was to bomba y plena what Duke Ellington was to jazz. Bomba y plena is the name of Puerto Rican folk music. Bomba is derived strongly from African drum rhythms and plena is a combination of Spanish and African sounds.

Rafael Cortijo began his career playing the conga, then later changed to the *timbales* (drums). Cortijo formed his combo in the early 1950s, at a time when Puerto Rican musicians were copying the popular Cuban sounds. Cortijo and his combo had a distinctly Puerto Rican sound and brought it to the height of commercial success. They played together for ten years and had a successful career as the most popular composers, arrangers, and interpreters of bomba y plena.

Cortijo died in New York in 1983.

Ismael Rivera, the combo's lead singer, was called *"El sonero mayor"* (The best Latin singer). With his husky voice and improvisational style, he set a new standard of musicianship. After leaving the combo, he formed his own band, "Los Cachimbos," and had many hits. He died in Puerto Rico in 1987.

In 1988 a park was opened in San Juan—La plaza de los salseros—to honor these two men.

Sammy Ayala was the percussionist for the band. He also provided the background vocals (*coro*) for the distinctive call and response in bomba y plena music. Sammy also composed some of the music. He remains active in the Puerto Rican music scene.